A LOVE IMPOSSIBLE

ROSIE CHAPEL

A Love Impossible

Rosie Chapel

First printing: 2020
ISBN: 978-0-6488365-8-2 (ebook)
ISBN: 978-0-6488365-9-9 (paperback)

Ulfire Pty. Ltd.
P.O. Box 1481
South Perth
WA 6951
Australia

www.rosiechapel.com

Cover Image: Courtesy of Period Images and Deposit Photos
Cover Designed by Lisa Miller with Got You Covered

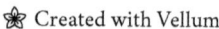 Created with Vellum

To all who refuse to allow others to dictate their choices, and who are prepared to risk everything for love...
...this is for you!

A Love Impossible

PROLOGUE

LONDON ~ MAY 1817

A door swung open silently and a dark shadow slipped into a study. Green eyes scanned the room. Finn Brennan's mouth curled in abhorrence at the opulent furnishings. Large, polished oak desk, a high-backed chair tucked in behind it, a fire laid but not lit.

Several potted plants scattered about, softened the heavy decor, but not enough to make the room feel either welcoming, or a place one might be comfortable working.

The safe should be behind the portrait in the alcove. Finn crept across the study, careful not to bang into the furniture. He reached the alcove and stared at the painting. He shuddered; this family had some of the ugliest ancestors he had ever seen… if indeed they were family portraits.

Swallowing his distaste, their beauty or lack thereof was not his concern, Finn lifted down the picture, and leant it against the wall.

There it was, in all its metallic glory. He smiled and got to work.

Within seconds, Finn found what he came for. Wrapped in a soft cloth, inside a tube fashioned from thick vellum and protected by a piece of the finest cotton, nestled his objective. Unwilling to tarry any longer than necessary, Finn simply slid it into the roll of canvas created for the purpose before tucking it into a specially made pocket in his knapsack.

Closing the safe, he re-hung the portrait and left the study exactly as he found it... well almost. Less than three feet from the passageway, which led to the back door and Finn's point of exit, a figure loomed up in front of him. Finn smothered a curse and pressed his back against the wall, hoping to avoid notice. No such luck. A candle was raised, and Finn recognised the face peering into the darkness.

It was Harold Prestwich, Earl of Ravensgarth; owner of the house he was in, and a man entirely lacking in morals, ethics and scruples. His reputation as an 'acquirer' of valuable artefacts through questionable channels, well-known yet unproven. He was tolerated by his peers, detested by his family and hated by his staff. A man, in fact, with little to redeem him.

There was a sharp intake of breath.

"What the devil?"

The flickering light moved towards Finn, who was trying to blend into the shadows. *Dammit all to hell.* He could not chance the earl preventing his escape. Removing his knife from its sheath, concealed beneath his black coat, Finn skirted around Ravensgarth's bulk and, instilling a malevolent edge to his voice, spoke in undertones.

"Go back to your bed and no one gets hurt."

Ravensgarth was not so easily scared and spun on his heel. "Well, well, well! What do we have here? Hmmmm? A nasty little thief, skulking around my home at two in the morning? I daresay I have every right to run you through." The earl's voice reflected his fury and Finn had to act quickly, or everything they had worked for would be lost.

"I asked nicely. Now find your bed, or I will have no alternative but to shut you up."

"You vile excuse of humanity." Ignorant of the irony of his words, Ravensgarth lurched to one side, and Finn realised he was reaching for one of the vicious looking swords displayed on the wall. A series of crude oaths ran though Finn's head.

This was not how it was supposed to go.

He had been given his orders. He was to let nothing, absolutely nothing, stand in his way of retrieving the treasure, and if that meant extreme measures were required, so be it. He took a breath; this wasn't the first time he had gone above and beyond and doubted it would be his last. In all honesty, he was doing the world a favour.

"I warned you." He hissed, and before the earl could react, Finn slit his throat from ear to ear. Warm blood frothed, spraying in random arcs across the walls, the floor and Finn, as the earl panicked.

Ravensgarth clutched at his neck, but there was nothing he could do. There was a ghastly gurgling sound as his body crumpled to the carpet, his limbs twitching as his heart tried to keep a man already dead, alive.

Finn held his breath, all was silent; no inquisitive footman or maid coming to check on their master. He waited for long moments, just to be certain, then stole along to the tradesmen's entrance, melting into the night as though he had never been there.

CHAPTER 1

DUBLIN ~ JUNE 1817

*E*dward Lindsay stood at the prow of the three-masted barque, watching the grey mass ahead of him increase the closer they sailed. The five-day journey from the Pool of London had been relatively smooth, and Captain Richards affirmed they should be docking in *Calafort Átha Cliath*, or Dublin Port by day's end — tide willing.

Edward was accompanying his adopted sister, Justina, to her aunt's home in Dublin. At least, that was the official reason for his visit. In reality, he had been tasked with hunting a killer.

While no one mourned the Earl of Ravensgarth's death, four weeks past, he *was* a peer of the realm, who *had* been viciously murdered and, it was later discovered, robbed.

Curiously, only one item was stolen and, although not considered intrinsically valuable, its historical significance was incalculable. An illuminated manuscript, dated to the period when Dublin was an ecclesiastical settlement, around the time of the Viking invasion.

Thought to have been in possession of the Kavanagh

family since its creation approximately nine hundred years ago, it detailed the founding of the settlement. The two names associated with its origins, *Duiblinn* and *Dyflin* — old Irish and old Norse respectively, meaning Black Pool — both appeared in the manuscript, which had vanished following a brazen robbery five months previously.

Although the Kavanaghs' Henrietta Street property was ransacked, little was taken. Four silver platters, two pearl-handled, flintlock pistols, a few pieces of jewellery, a quantity of coin — and the manuscript. This latter was the most shocking for the family, the loss of the other items inconsequential in comparison with the theft of the manuscript.

Every avenue of investigation came up empty, then about two months ago, whispers of a rare artefact began to circulate. An object of immeasurable cultural and historical importance. The people for whom Edward worked, began discreet enquiries. Ravensgarth's name cropped up too many times to be ignored.

A plan to have one of their number pose as a dealer in antiquities and be introduced to the earl as a prospective buyer was being set up, when Ravensgarth was murdered. The manuscript disappeared again, only to reappear in Dublin — in the possession of its rightful owner — two weeks later.

By sheer coincidence, Justina was travelling to Dublin, to spend the summer with her cousins. Once aware, Lucas Withers — Edward's boss — could not let this opportunity slip by. Edward would travel as Justina's guardian. His presence would not be unexpected — Dublin was a place Edward and his family often visited, and he was well-known and liked among the gentry.

Fortuitously, one of Lucas' associates happened to be good friends with the owner of a shipyard, persuading the latter to allow two extra passengers on a sea trial they were running.

Resting his elbows on the rail, Edward mulled over his instructions. They sounded very simple in the cool office on Bow Street. Listen, learn, and report and, in truth, he was eminently capable of coaxing people to reveal things they would never dream of telling a living soul.

He relished the challenge of uncovering secrets, and although he accepted it could be hazardous, that wasn't what was causing his stomach to tighten as they approached landfall.

Dublin held more than just a murderer.

There was also Aidan.

The regular swish of the waves against the side of the barque created a soothing rhythm and unbidden, Edward's mind wandered back to the first time he met Aidan Griffen.

It was six years ago, December. Edward was staying at his Aunt Agatha's — well, she was Viscount Mayhew's sister, which made her a kind of adopted aunt, Edward's connection being somewhat convoluted.

Serena and Jonathon Mayhew, along with their three children, were spending the winter months in Dublin because Agatha was about to give birth to her fifth child, and Serena wanted to be there in support. Liam Mackenna, Agatha's husband, was a good man, but Serena knew he would struggle to cope during Agatha's confinement.

Edward tagged along under sufferance. He had recently come down from Oxford, and Serena decided a complete break was in order. He had become withdrawn during the last year, his reserve worrying her.

She thought she knew what plagued him, but did not want to broach the subject, preferring that Edward reach out to her when he was ready. Since their arrival in Dublin, with no pressures, no exams, and no call on his time, Edward's normally open, and friendly personality had resurfaced.

While their parents were otherwise occupied, Edward allowed his two sisters and their older cousins to drag him into the city, or to one of the parks, or for a walk along the river.

When not acting as escort, he could be found buried in a book in the Mackenna's library, or with Jonathan and Liam at one of the gentleman's clubs; where he might indulge in a little light gambling or just sit and chat about what was going on in the world.

One afternoon, about a week before Christmas, Edward was sitting on a bench in the park the children declared was their absolute *favourite* — possibly to do with the number of wild animals who called it home. It was very cold, and the sky was heavy, snow was in the offing.

The inclement weather had kept the children indoors for a week and today was their first chance to get outside and expend some of their pent-up energy. Bundled up in winter cloaks, they were dashing about, playing with hoops and skipping ropes — oblivious to the fact it was considered an unseemly activity for young ladies.

Edward was laughing at Justina, who had fallen head first into a pile of snow, when he heard footsteps. Half-expecting it to be Serena or Jonathon, he turned, a ready smile on his lips.

The person coming towards him seemed vaguely familiar, but Edward couldn't place him. As the tall stranger drew level, he turned and nodded. Edward caught a glimpse of bright blue eyes, and a wild mop of black hair under the man's beaver.

"You'll be of the London folk staying with the Mackennas?" The question was flung out casually. Edward angled his head, the better to see the speaker.

"I am," he affirmed, slightly puzzled, unsure where this was going.

"Strange time of the year to visit. You should come in the summer. 'Tis beautiful then so 'tis."

"Family business," Edward replied rather curtly, unwilling to offer further details to someone he had never met.

"Sorry, I should introduce meself, I'm Aidan, Aidan Griffen. We live near the Mackennas. Our families are good friends."

Edward realised why Aidan seemed familiar, he had seen him in the neighbourhood. He recalled Liam mentioning Ruaidhrí and Márie Griffen — officially, the Earl and Countess of Middleham, although they rarely used their title — with fondness.

"Pleased to meet you, Aidan Griffen. I'm Edward Lindsay." He caught a frown, and guessed his lack of title, along with a surname different from Viscount Mayhew's, might confuse. "It's a long and very boring story, I might tell you one day." He grinned suddenly, glad when Aidan responded in kind.

That was the first of many meetings. During the next four years, they became close friends, and Edward concurred with Aidan — summer in Dublin was most congenial. If either wanted more, it was never discussed; such admissions were dangerous, not to mention against the law.

Edward's visits to Ireland were fleeting, his life was in London, Aidan's in Dublin. The distance was too great, and what was the point anyway? They had no future. Edward's last trip was over two years ago and, never expecting to return, had done everything in his power to forget the handsome Irishman, but as the boat sailed into port, he knew he was deluding himself.

CHAPTER 2

*E*dward shook himself out of his reverie and went to find Justina. She was in her cabin, luggage neatly stacked by the door.

"We're about to dock, are you ready?" he asked, grinning at her eager face.

He knew why she was so excited about arriving in Dublin. During the voyage, Justina had confessed she hoped a certain Alastar Whelan — a young man from a respectable family, with whom Justina had been friends since both were children — might be bold enough to ply his suit. Edward was aware they had been exchanging letters for years. Justina, wanting a male perspective and not daring to discuss it with her protective father, occasionally asked Edward's advice regarding some of Alastar's remarks.

Edward was pleased to be consulted. His position in this family was unusual; he was no blood relation to any of the Mayhew family, yet Serena treated him as her son. Edward had become the ward of her first husband, Winston — Edward's uncle — upon the death of his natural parents almost immediately after his birth.

Winston died when Edward was seven-years-old, and Serena remarried two years later. Her new husband Jonathon Cardon, Viscount Mayhew, welcomed the little boy without reserve. Two decades and two daughters later, they were the only family Edward knew, and they loved him unconditionally, a sentiment he reciprocated.

Justina and her younger sister, Winifred, thought the sun shone out of Edward. He might be ten years their senior, but he was never stuffy like some of their friends' older brothers. He always had time for them and could be relied upon to act the goat should any given situation demand frivolity.

"Of course, I am looking forward to seeing Aunt Agatha and my cousins again." Her prim reply was belied by the sparkle in her eye.

"Come on then, grab your valise. Tom will see to the rest of our trunks, if he can find a cart big enough..." he let that dangle. Justina had packed luggage for three years never mind three months.

"Edward!" She shoved him in the shoulder and the siblings teased each other as they walked out on deck. Dublin Port came into view, the sounds and smells of a bustling dock floated towards them on the breeze.

Edward closed his eyes and inhaled. Half of him hoped he could unearth the perpetrator in a week, the other half wanted it to be a protracted investigation, however painful that might prove.

Three hours later, having thanked Captain Richards and the crew for making their voyage so comfortable, Edward and Justina, their few staff and huge pile of luggage — nearly all Justina's — arrived at Upper Mount Street.

The door flew open and footmen flowed out in a veritable wave to collect their belongings and usher them into the house. Mr Trimble, the butler, announced them and Justina fairly bounced across the room to hug her aunt. Edward followed more sedately, only to be enfolded into a warm embrace by the lady of the house.

"My, Edward, I do believe you have grown again." Agatha peered up at him.

Edward grinned. "No, Aunt Agatha, 'tis you who is shrinking. You'll soon be able to run wild with the leprechauns." The same greeting they exchanged every time they met and Edward suffered the usual elbow jabbed in his side. "Hello, Aunt, how are you? Mama and Papa send their warmest regards and beg to know when you will visit them in London."

"Maybe one day." Agatha smiled and patted his cheek, as though he was eight not eight and twenty. "I hear you had quite the adventure last year. You must tell me all about it, but right now, I imagine you might like to freshen up after so many days at sea." She rang the bell and instructed the maid to organise hot baths for their guests. "Dinner will be at seven, we eat early here, and drinks will be served on the terrace, when you're ready."

That evening, once Justina had retired, Edward gave his aunt and uncle an abridged version of what happened the previous year. A man in the employ of Serena's brother-in-law, whose determination to acquire status, had almost ended in the deaths of three people, Edward included.

Instrumental in uncovering his identity, Edward's efforts were rewarded when Lucas Withers offered him a position in his covert organisation. The work was interesting and sometimes perilous, but Edward thrived on it.

His aunt and uncle listened attentively, then Liam remarked, shrewdly,

"Are we to suppose your reason for accompanying Justina is not simply because you like Dublin in June?"

Edward felt unaccustomed heat wash up his cheeks. "You suppose correctly. Did you read about the murder of Lord Ravensgarth?" They both nodded, and Edward, after extracting their word the details would remain confidential, explained the reason for his visit. He concluded, "they suspect 'tis someone in the employ of the gentry, probably the Kavanaghs. Not..." he raised his palms placatingly as Liam started to defend his friend, "... that I necessarily believe Kavanagh is behind it, but someone close to him could be.

"The whereabouts of the manuscript is the least of my worries, 'tis the murderer I am interested in. Most are glad the manuscript is back with the person it was stolen from in the first place. 'Tis a family heirloom, whatever its significance, historically. We are investigating the murder. Regardless of whether Ravensgarth orchestrated the original theft, and however much he was disliked, murder is murder."

Agatha and Liam nodded their understanding and the discussion went back and forth for a little longer, then Edward, tired after days of travel, excused himself and went to bed.

"Aye, well I hope he realises it won't be easy," Liam said after the door had closed behind their nephew.

"Edward is no idiot, Liam, and he is well known to folk around here. They will open up to him without realising it. He'll not want to cause any more upset than he has to, but he's right, a murderer cannot be allowed to walk free. There are rules, whether we like them or not, and society would soon deteriorate into anarchy if people broke them without consequence. 'Tis a slippery slide," Agatha countered sagely, before turning the conversation to the much less sombre topic of their youngest child's latest exploits, which kept them amused until slumber called.

CHAPTER 3

Over the next few days, Edward visited those he knew in the neighbourhood. Ostensibly re-establishing his acquaintance, in reality seeing what information he could wheedle out of them.

Whispers, rumours, a vague theory or innuendo. So far, he had not heard anything particularly useful, although without fail, everyone with whom he spoke considered the death of the earl a just comeuppance for stealing the manuscript in the first place. His guilt — incontrovertible.

It was also patently obvious everyone knew the value of the artefact, both as an historical source — detailing the monumental changes wrought by the Norse invaders — and monetarily. The more people he spoke with, the more Edward began to hope he might *not* be able to find the guilty party.

Towards the end of his first week in Dublin, Edward and Justina, along with the rest of the Mackenna family, were invited to a party at the Whelans' beautiful home. Justina had already enjoyed several constitutionals and one carriage ride with Alastar, and it was clear their youthful affection had blossomed into something enduring.

While they were preparing for the party, Justina took Edward into her confidence.

"I think Alastar might ask to speak with you tonight. Are you happy to act on behalf of Papa?" Justina asked as she straightened Edward's cravat, brushing non-existent fluff off the dark green of his jacket. "There now, you look very handsome. You'll be much sought after."

Edward forced a smile and bowed. "I will do my utmost to behave as Lord Mayhew would expect." His formal affirmation making Justina giggle. "Thank you for your help. Now we must hurry, or we shall never get there, and then what would Alastar think?"

Two hours later, Edward was standing in the corner of the Whelans' drawing room chatting with Donal Kavanagh, a nobleman from an ancient Irish lineage. Aunt Agatha, who felt it her duty to acquaint Edward with a detailed history of Dublin's gentry, had explained the Kavanaghs' rather complex status.

Traditionally, Donal Kavanagh would have been referred to as *Ard Tiana* or high lord, but this moniker seemingly confused the English, who bestowed on a recent — and by recent, Agatha meant almost two centuries earlier — ancestor, the title Marquis of Downe.

This was the man whose family owned the manuscript and into whose hands it had been returned. The marquis was an affable gentleman and despite his age — he was nearing eighty years old — was still sharp as a rapier. They had been talking for about fifteen minutes when Kavanagh said.

"We need to stop prevaricating. Yes, I have the

manuscript back. It is in a place no one will think to look. No, I cannot tell you who retrieved it, and even if I did know I would probably not disclose their identity. I am inordinately thankful someone cared enough to find it, no I did not ask them to, and am saddened a death occurred because if it.

"What I will say, Mr Lindsay, is that this is my heritage. I am descended from Irish kings, and my family have been custodians of the manuscript for centuries. As far as I am concerned the subject is closed. I wish you the best of luck in unmasking the murderer, but I am not in any position to assist your endeavours."

Edward smiled grimly. "I appreciate your honesty. I confess, my heart is not wholly vested in my task, but whatever my feelings, the person broke the law and if I can find them, I will not hesitate to bring them to justice..." he paused, "... whatever that might mean."

Donal Kavanagh appraised Edward for a long moment, then nodded his head as though coming to a decision. "If I hear anything pertinent, I shall send you a message."

"That is all I ask. Thank you, sir." Edward bowed and the two shook hands. Donal strode off towards a group of businessmen engaged in a heated discussion about some political issue.

Edward, relieved not to talk for a while, leant against the wall. He was not one for parties and hoped Whelan would approach him sooner rather than later, then he could quietly slip away. About to seek another glass of whiskey, he was stayed by a hand on his arm.

"Well, well, if it isn't Mr Edward Lindsay, last seen departing these shores two years ago. I never thought I'd clap eyes on you again, yet here ye are in all yer glory."

It was Aidan.

Edward stared at the hand curled around his sleeve and felt his stomach muscles clench. Even the sight of Aidan's long fingers was enough to render him incapable. He lifted his head and strove for nonchalance.

"Aidan, you're looking well." Edward was impressed his voice sounded firm, with just the right amount of interest, while he allowed himself the luxury of admiring the man in front of him.

Edward would not be surprised if Aidan was descended from the Fae, he never seemed to age. Not a line on his face, his hair — still as unruly, although currently restrained in a queue — was black as pitch, and his eyes the brightest blue Edward had ever seen. He knew he could not avoid Aidan and, if he was honest, wasn't even sure he wanted to. The ache in the region of his heart worth it for a few moments in his company. *Pathetic you are, Edward*, he chastised himself inwardly.

"How's life in the big city?" Aidan enquired, politely.

"It has its ups and downs." Edward offered the ghost of a smile.

"Are you still employed by Lord Rycote?"

"Only periodically. There was a bit of an incident last year, which resulted in me joining a government organisation. 'Tis absorbing work."

"Is that why you're here?" Aidan studied Edward speculatively. Edward pondered his answer. It wasn't that he didn't trust Aidan, but Dublin was a tight-knit community, he didn't want them to close ranks before he had the chance to investigate every possible lead.

"I am here as guardian to Justina. Papa was unable to spare the time, so I came in his stead. I do believe she's expecting young Whelan to show his hand." Neatly evading a direct answer.

"'Tis about time," Aidan countered, "those two have been enamoured for years."

The initial awkwardness of their meeting, aided by another tot or two of whiskey, slowly dissipated and before long the two men were chatting as though Edward had never left Dublin.

Whelan did pluck up the courage to speak to Edward, who affirmed he was pleased to approve the young man's suit. Justina's joy was plain to see and, watching the couple together, Edward knew there would be a more official approach before she departed Dublin in September.

As the evening wore on, the party became quite riotous, prompting Edward to slip away from the revelry and venture onto the terrace which overlooked the back garden. It was blessedly tranquil.

The sky was beginning to darken; remnants of the flaming sunset now morphing through shades of deep purple. The air was clear, the tang from the sea wafting in on the gentle breeze. Edward inhaled a long breath and tilted his head back to admire the vast heavens.

CHAPTER 4

"*R*unning away?" A figure hovered at the far end of the terrace.

The quiet question had Edward's head snapping around. Aidan.

"What prompted that?"

"Ah, now we are deflecting."

Edward ran his hand around the back of his neck. "No, I am not deflecting. I want to know. What makes you think I have any reason to run away?"

"It's what you do best."

"Not fair and you know it." He could not keep having the same argument. When Edward left Dublin, two years previously, Aidan had accused him of being spineless, of taking the easy option. *Easy!* The man had no idea just how difficult it was to walk away.

Aidan's parents — their eldest son's marriage probably arranged before his birth — announced his betrothal, expecting Aidan to set aside his own wishes for duty. Edward simply could not be there when Aidan wed a suitable young lady to please his parents, endlessly thankful Serena and

Jonathon knew, accepted, and left him alone. He would remain a bachelor. It was not so uncommon these days.

"How is Orla?" He was amazed his voice was steady.

Aidan moved out of the shadows. "She is beautiful as ever. Her first child is due within the next month or so."

Edward felt as though he had been punched and actually bent slightly to counteract the pain. *No! He wasn't prepared, he would never be prepared. Why, oh why had he returned to Dublin?* Running away sounded rather inviting right about now.

"Her husband is over the moon." Aidan sounded positively gleeful.

"C-congratulations." Edward almost gagged on the words and, unable to look Aidan in the eye, turned, his heel grinding over the flagstones of the terrace. "I am very happy for you. Excuse me." He willed his legs to obey his bidding, intent on leaving with as much dignity as possible.

Aidan grabbed Edward's arm as he passed, preventing his flight. Edward glared and tried to wrench free, but Aidan tightened his grip. He leant so close his breath brushed Edward's ear, making his skin prickle.

"Do not jump to conclusions, my friend. Orla married Ciarán."

Edward jerked backwards and searched Aidan's eyes, midnight blue in the waning light, unable to decide whether this was good or bad. Yes, it was good in that Aidan was not yet wed, but were his parents still ruling his future?

"I... I... what about...? How...? Because..." Edward clamped his mouth shut; the several whiskeys he had consumed dulling his brain. A tiny flicker of hope sparked into life, then just as quickly died. What did it matter anyway? He would leave, Aidan would stay.

"I ought to say I am sorry, offer trite platitudes, or some such nonsense but my regret would be feigned. I am selfish enough to hope you do not wed, shameful though it is, but as you rightfully pointed out, it has been two years. A long time to hold onto a dream." A red stain coloured Edward's cheeks, and this time he managed to disentangle himself.

"Did you?" Aidan held his gaze and, for the life of him, Edward could not look away.

"Did I what?"

"Hold onto a dream."

About to deny it, Edward hesitated. *Dare he…?* Straightening his shoulders, he bared his soul. "'Tis all I have."

He heard an odd sound, like a kind of strangled groan — then it happened.

Aidan's lips crashed against his.

It was not their first kiss but might well be their last.

Stunned, Edward's mind reeled. This was madness! If anyone came out onto the terrace they were doomed, but even the fear of discovery could not stop his response. Deliberately quashed and tortuously familiar emotions began to ripple through him. Kissing Aidan was like coming home, for although they had never taken the ultimate step, Edward knew the other man's body as well as he knew his own.

He knew about the long scar on Aidan's left arm, caused by a branch when he fell out of a tree as a child. He knew about the birthmark on his right hip. He knew where to touch him to elicit a desired reaction, and he knew exactly where each muscle on his taut physique began and ended. All this was etched into his mind, where it would remain forever.

Their time together was, would always be, short-lived. Their love, if indeed it was love, could never be acknowledged, celebrated, enjoyed. He could scarcely expect Aidan to put his life on hold for the impossible — it was unfair, nay, cruel. His head screamed at him to stop, at the same time as one hand slid around Aidan's waist, and the other cupped the nape of his neck, fingers grasping the once neat queue, like a lifeline.

Tongues battled for dominance, while their limbs met and melded — Aidan tasted of whiskey and pipe tobacco, and Edward craved it like a suffocating man craves air. Nothing else mattered. The kiss deepened, became less desperate and more languorous, while hands roamed; fingers relishing the contact.

White heat licked along Edward's veins, his heart pounded, and he questioned, briefly, whether the world had stopped, and the two of them were trapped between moments. He wanted to cling onto it, to luxuriate in the tumult of sensations, but even as the thought skirted his mind, laughter shattered the quiet and the two men jolted apart as though stung.

By the time several guests spilled through the French doors, Aidan and Edward were at opposite ends of the terrace. Edward was perched on the stone balustrade, his back to a fluted pillar, while Aidan was sitting on a wrought iron bench overlooking the garden — to all appearances, strangers.

The following day, nursing a thumping head and a serious case of the grumps, Edward took himself out for a long walk. Justina offered to accompany him but, after thanking her, explained he needed some time alone.

He had been in Dublin a week; he was no closer to uncovering a murderer than he had been before he left London and, had done precisely what he'd instructed himself not to do. He was tempted to slap his forehead, but it ached too badly.

He made his way to the Liffey, the river which ran through the town, and strolled along its banks for a good hour. The sun was warm, prompting him to shrug out of his jacket and untie his cravat. To stay dressed in formal attire seemed almost an insult to such glorious weather.

An azure sky was punctuated by a smattering of white fluffy clouds. The air was clean and fresh — much fresher than London at this time of year, which tended to be stifling throughout the summer months. Gentle sounds drifted on the breeze; the distant clang of the docks, faint laughter — children probably — birds chirping, and insects droning. They were comfortable sounds, welcoming — June in Ireland was perfection.

Edward's ankle, broken the previous year during the incident he had mentioned to his aunt and uncle, began to throb, and he availed himself of a convenient bench. Resting his elbows on his knees, hands loosely clasped between his legs, he watched the ducks paddling.

So peaceful.

The soft swish of the river as it flowed along, the muted calls of the water fowl while they foraged in the moss and reeds, the rustle of leaves, the dappled light through the trees creating intricate patterns across the ground.

He wished his mind was as tranquil.

After Aidan and he were disturbed on the terrace the previous evening, they went their separate ways. Neither spoke to the other again, and Edward, concerned his involuntary reactions to Aidan would give him away, made his excuses and left before midnight.

He accepted his behaviour bordered on cowardly, and despite the obvious ardour between them, was left floundering. Did Aidan want a fling? Edward was not sure he could handle that, but what else could either of them offer? Wasn't it better just to ensure they had no further contact until he had completed his investigation?

Would his heart survive another goodbye?

CHAPTER 5

*O*f course, it would — Edward was not naïve, nor was he given to fanciful notions about love and loss, but he remembered how long it took for him to come to terms with leaving Aidan two years ago.

It was as though, every time he left Dublin another piece of his heart stayed. *Soon you will be naught but a husk,* he thought, then grinned to himself; *tsk, you are being far too melodramatic, Edward Lindsay, where is your fortitude?*

He rested his back against the bench and closed his eyes, letting the serenity of the afternoon surround and calm him. Rather than dwell on what couldn't be altered, Edward turned his mind to the investigation. It was increasingly unlikely, even if the culprit was in Dublin, he would uncover his identity. Whoever had broken into Ravensgarth's home was an expert; if the earl had not disturbed his murderer, the theft would have gone unnoticed until someone had reason to open the safe.

Did this mean the same thief had broken into other homes in London, or were his activities confined to Dublin, and this was an exception? Was it purely because of the manuscript? Edward mulled over this.

If members of the *ton* had been subject to a spate of break-ins, their instinct would be to hush it up, but among trusted friends at Whites or Boodle's or any of the private clubs, discussion would be more candid. Many who worked for Lucas were nobility, and thus frequented the clubs, where garnering information required little effort — casual chit-chat overheard, or a trusted steward with his ear to the ground.

Edward contemplated whether it was worth sending a letter to Lucas asking whether any similar burglaries had taken place, eventually discounting it. He would be back in London soon, he could follow it up then, if necessary. If whoever was behind this was currently in Dublin, he wasn't robbing houses in London.

Frustrated at the complete lack of anything tangible, Edward put it out of his head. Uncaring how it looked, he swung his legs around to lie full length along the bench, bunched up his jacket to form a pillow, folded his arms over his chest and dozed.

An hour later, this was how Aidan found him. The Irishman, doing much the same as Edward, was walking off a hang-over. Avoiding Edward after their encounter on the terrace, had proved difficult. Every time Aidan caught sight of the tall, dark-haired Londoner, he was drawn towards him. Finally, he joined a card game, and knocked back a decent number of whiskeys in an effort to distract himself.

He noticed when Edward had left, a little before midnight, and was tempted to follow. The cloak of darkness would be enough to shield an assignation, but he refrained.

Now he wished he had ignored his brain and listened to his heart.

Aidan knew Edward's time in Dublin was limited but remained confused as to why he had come in the first place. His explanation that he was here in Lord Mayhew's stead did not quite ring true. Aidan could read Edward and recognised certain nuances in his behaviour. The man was hiding something… but what?

He scuffed along the banks of the Liffey, engrossed in his thoughts. As he approached one of the benches, placed at random intervals along the path, he heard a gentle snore. Presuming it was a tramp, or one of the town drunks sleeping it off, he was about to continue past — disturbing them was never a good idea — when he glanced down.

Recognising the snoozing gentleman — head pillowed on a rolled-up jacket, waistcoat unbuttoned, shirt coming untucked, and cravat loosened, Aidan swallowed a chuckle. Stretching over the frame of the bench, he shook Edward's shoulder.

Edward was lost in dreams, his foot ached abominably, and he felt dizzy. All he wanted was to sleep, but the hand rocking his shoulder was relentless as were the demands he wake up. The image of a fair-haired woman popped into his head, along with the impression of a dark, dank space.

"Miss Truscott, is it your avowed intent to disturb my rest?" Edward muttered; eyes still closed.

"Miss Truscott, hmmm? Pray tell me, who is this lady intent on rousing you?"

The pretty face swam in front of him, but the voice did not sound right. Much too deep. Groaning, Edward peeled back his eyelids and squinted into the sunlight. Still slightly disoriented, he frowned at the person looming over him.

It wasn't Lucy Truscott. Where the dickens was he? Then his brain caught up. He was in Dublin and here was the one person for whose company he yearned, but who common sense dictated he avoid.

"Aidan. Sorry, I was…" he stopped.

"Dreaming about a certain Miss Truscott, apparently." Aidan sounded both amused and curious.

"'Tis a long story."

"I have time…" Aidan hooked a hand under Edward's legs and lifted them off the bench, sitting in their place, "…if you have the inclination to share."

Edward shuffled upright and along until there was a gap between them. He ran a hand through his hair, a rich-brown lock falling over his forehead. He saw Aidan's hand rise, then fall. Pushing aside the emotion the gesture evoked, Edward explained what had occurred the previous year.

"And Miss Truscott?"

"Is happily married to her William."

"Is this why you walk with a slight limp?" Aidan quizzed.

"Yes, the doctor did his best to set my ankle, but it remains a little stiff, and causes some discomfort if I am tired or in very cold weather."

"Am I to assume this is the 'bit of an incident' you mentioned last evening? The one which led to your current employment?"

Edward nodded.

"Why are you really here, Edward?" Aidan's question hung between them. "'Tis nothing to do with Justina and Alastar is it?"

Edward twisted so he could look Aidan in the eye. "I cannot divulge that information yet. I promise to do so at the earliest opportunity, but at the moment 'tis safer for you not to know."

"'Tis serious then?"

"Very." Edward stared out across the river. "Do you trust me?"

Silence.

Edward held his breath.

"With my life."

Edward blew a sigh. "Thank you. I truly wish I could tell yo—"

"Do not think on it *mo chara*." Aidan's lilting accent coiled around the words — *my friend*.

"Are we friends?" Edward ventured.

"We are so much more, but it is a good start." Aidan winked.

Something had shifted during their conversation. Edward couldn't quite put his finger on what it was, but suddenly, he felt as though invisible tethers had slackened and the weight pressing down on his shoulders was decreasing.

He had no idea what their future held, but all at once, he wanted to explore the possibility of a maybe. Did Aidan want that too? They had spent six years resisting what came as natural to them as breathing, and he no longer wanted to fight. He would take whatever Aidan could offer.

Almost giddy, Edward seized the moment. Reaching out, he slid his palm under Aidan's, curling his fingers around those of the Irishman, gratified when he felt Aidan reciprocate. Edward stared at their clasped hands, then lifted his gaze to Aidan — mahogany on cobalt

"*Mo ghrá thú.*" Edward knew his grasp of Gaelic was sketchy, but he was given to understand from Justina that *mo ghrá thú* meant, 'you are my beloved'.

Aidan's eyes widened in shock and Edward experienced a rush of panic. Surely, he hadn't misread the situation. Not after six years, not after that kiss. He opened his mouth to retract the words, to apologise, when he felt Aidan's fingers squeeze his.

Edward felt a beam as wide as the river they sat beside begin to curve his mouth and, forgetting they were in the middle of a public footpath and anyone could happen upon them, closed the gap and brushed his lips to Aidan's.

CHAPTER 6

*S*ince their declarations on the banks of the Liffey, Edward and Aidan had taken every opportunity to meet. Their behaviour towards each other did not, could not, change and to outward appearances seemed no more than casual acquaintances. The occasional touch had to suffice and, except for one stolen and very passionate kiss in the obscurity of a gloomy corridor, they managed to control their desires.

In the midst of all this, Edward was still working to unearth anything relating to the person who snatched the manuscript from Ravensgarth House. To that end he decided to eschew the clubs frequented by the gentry and loiter around some of the more questionable areas of Dublin. Taverns and bawdy houses were known as much for the gossip a person might overhear as they were for drink and... entertainment.

Attired in the practical and well-worn clothing, preferred by the working class, Edward augmented his disguise by scrubbing his hands with dirt and burying his nails in the black loam of the Mackenna's garden beds. He also smeared some across his face and down his neck, dusting off the excess, to make it look as though he had come straight from the fields or a factory. The final touch — a bit of chalk crushed and rubbed over his head, giving his normally clean hair a greyish cast, and Edward was almost unrecognisable.

Liam and Agatha concealed their shock at their nephew's scruffy appearance — accepting his word, he would take every care — with remarkable aplomb.

"I am cognisant of the dangers drinking houses present. I will not stay long," Edward assured Agatha when his aunt questioned his sanity.

"Wait, lad," Liam interjected, an idea coming to him, "let me get Declan to accompany ye. Two is safer than one and he is well known hereabouts."

Although eager to be on his way, Edward could see the sense in this and acceded to his uncle's request. It was another half-an-hour before he and Declan — one of Liam's footmen — left the house, heading north across the new footbridge spanning the Liffey.

The sun was just dropping below the horizon. Long shadows created a sombre aspect to once elegant streets, slowly falling into disrepair following the decision by many of the gentry to move south of the river. Edward and Declan chatted while they walked, the latter providing the former with tips and caveats about the area for which they were aiming.

Edward could smell the taverns before they reached them, reminding him of similar establishments around London's rookeries and the docks. Oddly, the aroma made him feel slightly nostalgic for home — not that he visited such places, but the headquarters of the organisation he worked for was situated close by, and its operatives were regularly exposed to the underbelly of life.

Declan suggested they start their evening at the Dog and Gun and, as the two men shouldered their way through a crowd of drinkers, Declan was hailed by several customers. Tankards of the Dublin brewed dark porter in hand, they joined a group of Declan's friends. Declan introduced Edward as a distant cousin from England who had just started working as a gardener for the Mackennas. No one questioned his presence and, after he bought a round of drinks in thanks for their welcome, Edward was accepted as one of them.

This was a pattern he was to repeat for the next week or so. Declan and he ventured further into the maze of back streets, visiting gaming hells, all manner of drinking houses, and the occasional brothel.

Without giving himself away, Edward managed to convince Declan he would rather not avail himself of the bounty on offer at the bawdy houses, because he was affianced to a lovely young lady and did not want to risk catching anything.

Declan, who was usually completely foxed by this time, swallowed Edward's excuse without argument, to the latter's relief.

Twelve days, a *lot* of beer, and three evenings trying to become one with the furniture at a brothel, later — his coin rapidly diminishing, Edward's luck turned. He caught a snippet of pertinent information, the first tangible evidence the killer was here in Dublin.

He and Declan were drinking in O'Connoll's, a relatively decent alehouse, when three men to their right started arguing about a series of robberies. Doubtless the beer had deprived them of sense, for none tried to lower their voices, or maybe those in hearing range presumed their claims were bravado.

Listening carefully, Edward surmised they worked for a gentleman named Finn who, in their humble opinion was skimming too much from their ill-gotten gains and needed bringing down to size. In and of itself the conversation was meaningless, until one of them groused,

"'E's been uppity since he come back from London. Just because he were picked to do that job, thinks 'e's better than the rest of us, and look at the mess 'e left. Crows curse on 'im I say."

They all crossed themselves at this, making Edward bite his lip so as not to laugh. They could talk about theft and murder without so much as the blink of an eye, but utter a malediction against one of their own, and they needed divine protection.

His piece said, the originator of the discussion turned the conversation to other matters. Edward, however, was pleased with the night's efforts. It was barely a morsel, but he had a name. There could not be too many men in the vicinity named Finn, who had travelled to London recently.

Pretending to be inebriated to the point of insensibility, Edward stumbled towards the group, waving his tankard and talking as though to a companion, deliberately slurring his words and mimicking slang he knew to be peculiar to the north of England.

"No, no, no, get off me yer daft apeth, ish no time to go yet. The mishish will still be awake." Cackling with laughter at his own wit, he made sure he fell awkwardly against one of their number. They reacted as he hoped. Swearing, the man shoved him, but as Edward staggered away, he heard one of them grouse,

"Sean, Niall, let's go. Far too many eejits in 'ere tonight." His mates muttered an agreement, and knocked Edward flying in their haste to leave, ignoring his splutters and drunken oaths.

Picking himself up from the filthy floor, Edward's intoxicated demeanour vanished. He brushed himself down, supped the rest of his porter, motioned to Declan, and thanked the barkeep.

Once out into the cool of the evening, he mulled over what he'd heard. Declan had seen the three men on occasion, and admitted the name Finn sounded familiar, but that was all.

It would do for now. The thrill of the chase coiled through Edward. He was finally closing in.

CHAPTER 7

*J*t was almost midday before Edward roused. Long
nights trudging between bars had caught up with
him and he slept like the dead. Justina woke him by dint of
banging on the door of his bedchamber until she heard his
grumbled response.

"Come on Edward, stop lazing about. The day is too
glorious to waste."

"Go away and let a man sleep."

"Not a chance. Luncheon will be served shortly, then you
and I are taking a ride."

Justina reminded Edward of Lucy Truscott — now Lady
Blackthorne — unfailingly, and occasionally annoyingly,
cheerful. Both women always looked for the positives and
would do anything for someone they cared about. It was also
why he had not apprised Justina of the real reason he accompanied her to Dublin, knowing full well she would want to
assist in any way she could.

Giving up on slumber, Edward dragged himself out of
bed and, pulling on his banyan, yanked open the door,

catching Justina — who was leaning against it — before she sprawled on her backside.

"My eyes are open and I'm upright, are you satisfied?" He glared at his sister, who — wholly unrepentant — grinned back.

"Good, now get dressed and join us for lunch. This afternoon, 'tis just you and I. Uncle Liam has agreed to let us take the carriage, and I have organised a picnic."

Edward stared at her, still not fully awake. Justina, used to his abstracted behaviour, shoved him back into his room and shut the door, telling him he had twenty minutes, or she would be back.

A little later, after a light meal, Justina was ushering her brother into a waiting carriage. Declan, perched on the driver's seat, tipped his cap at Edward who greeted his drinking partner with a slap on the shoulder.

"Good afternoon, Declan. I had no idea you were groom as well as footman."

"Miss Cardon asked whether I would be so kind as to take the reins and 'tis a nice change of pace."

They chatted amicably as the carriage rattled through the streets, taking the road south, and it wasn't long before they were out of the city. The verdant countryside around Dublin flowed out ahead of them, drawing the eye towards the far distant Wicklow Mountains, the summer haze giving the impression they were floating in soft purple splendour.

"This view is sublime." Justina sighed in contentment. "Now, while we are enjoying so beautiful an afternoon, please tell me what you are up to."

"Up to?" Edward assumed his most innocent expression.

"Do not pretend you have no idea what I'm talking about,

Edward Lindsay," Justina tutted. "You have been out every night for nearly two weeks, often with poor Declan in tow." She waved her hand at the young footman who grinned. "You never do this. Moreover, I have long suspected this trip is more than just a holiday. I recall you saying, wild horses could not make you return to Dublin, so whatever prompted this visit must be important."

Edward studied Justina's face, noticing the stubborn lift of her chin and the narrowing of her gaze. He attempted to mollify her with a morsel of information.

"'Tis nothing need worry you. I am..." he hesitated, trying to find an explanation which might satisfy Justina without piquing her interest further. "... looking into something for Major Withers. It is a sensitive issue and requires a cautious approach."

His effort was in vain.

"To do with the murder of Lord Ravenscroft, I presume?"

Edward gaped, temporarily struck mute by her perception. "What makes you say that?" he asked when he got his mouth working again.

Justina shrugged. "The timing was too coincidental. You must consider me witless if you do not think I can put two and two together. I read about the earl's death in one of the broadsheets, you and Papa discussed it when you thought no one was listening, and it was all the gossip for weeks. I heard about the stolen manuscript and that it related to the founding of Dublin. Then, three weeks later, a month prior to our original departure date, behold, we are boarding one of Trentams' ships, bound for Dublin. Tell. Me. What. Is. Going. On." She spaced out each word with determined deliberation.

"Justina, I ca—"

"Do not dare say you cannot. Edward be sensible. If your investigation is risky and anything happens to you, what am

I supposed to tell our parents? You have no idea how worried they were last year during the Mr Garrick debacle." Justina had no qualms about playing on Edward's affection for his family. "Pleeeeeeease." She smiled winsomely and pressed her hand on his sleeve.

Edward gave up, and without revealing any information he deemed classified, provided his sister with a brief synopsis. "That is all I am prepared to say, and I think that is too much." His tones resigned.

"I am entrusting you with this only because you are correct, someone ought to know the details, just in case. However," he pinned her with his dark gaze, "to know leaves you vulnerable, so you must *not* repeat this to anyone, not even Alastar, do you understand? 'Tis confidential and I do not want to tip my hand. I believe, after last evening, I am close to identifying the killer. He will not want to be discovered and will likely do everything in his power to prevent it, making him dangerous."

He waited until Justina nodded her agreement. "That goes for you too, Declan." Edward glanced at the young man who had been his companion for most of his nightly sojourns. "You have been kind enough to assist my endeavours and I do not wish you to pay a price for that."

"My lips are sealed." Declan grinned. "My, but it's been entertaining. Your brother can talk the birds out of the trees, Miss Cardon. The things people have told him, much of which, I confess was better unsaid. Are you sure he's not Irish?"

"He always managed to persuade Winnie and me to spill our secrets, even when we flatly refused to," Justina chuckled. "Moreover, I would be proud to claim Irish ancestry. 'Tis a beautiful country and her people are so welcoming. I am hoping Dublin will feature rather prominently in my future," she added, with uncharacteristic shyness, her cheeks blushing a becoming shade of pink.

Edward patted her knee. "'Tis more than a hope, Justina. Now, enough of weighty talk, let us enjoy this marvellous afternoon. I do not want to miss this spectacular scenery. Did you say something about a picnic? Declan, you must join us..." pointing out a suitable place to sit under a sprawling oak tree, at the rise of a gentle hill from where they could see for miles.

No further mention was made of murder.

CHAPTER 8

*T*he next few days passed without incident, although Edward did begin to make discreet enquiries about the man called Finn who recently travelled to England, and who happened to be acquainted with a Sean and a Niall.

Initially he hit a proverbial brick wall, then one evening, when he was home alone, Edward received a surprise visitor. It was Donal Kavanagh. The elderly man looked fatigued, his normally ruddy complexion pale and his eyes shadowed.

The dramatic change in so short a time both concerned and puzzled Edward, who rose from his seat and greeted the nobleman with a bow. "Good evening, my lord. To what do I owe this honour? You seem… discomposed."

"I have heard rumours and am here to discuss their veracity."

"Please…" Edward, astonished at how fast word had reached the marquis, indicated one of the large wing-backed chairs. Grouped around the open French doors, their arrangement took advantage of the balmy evening air. "…would you care for a whiskey?"

Kavanagh nodded and once Edward had poured the amber spirit, he joined his guest, the two men sipping their drinks quietly.

"I understand you are looking for a man named Finn?" Kavanagh spoke after several minutes of companionable silence.

"I am indeed," Edward replied and, taking a gamble, explained why.

"Could it not be coincidence?"

"Of course, but their conversation implied they were involved in deception of one form or another and after their comment about this man Finn's recent visit to London, it was worth following up. It might lead to nothing, but it is all I have."

Edward opened his palms in a vaguely conciliatory gesture.

"My lord, I have no mind to hold an innocent man responsible, but this information is credible. I do not barge in like a herd of wild boar, I employ a variety of techniques to weed out the pertinent from the irrelevant. I have been doing this long enough to know the conversation I over-heard was significant. Moreover, my instinct tells me, if Finn is not the murderer, he knows who is," he paused, "and I always trust my instinct."

Donal Kavanagh heaved a tired sigh. "I have in my house-hold a man named Finn Brennan. He is the son of my wife's cousin and has been living with us for the past five years. I fear neither my conscience, nor my good lady wife, will let me rest until I have disclosed this to you. Perhaps you might visit Downe House, whereupon I will arrange for Finn to present himself for an interview."

Edward could see how hard it was for the marquis to speak thus. He was, in essence, betraying a member of his family. "My lord, I give you my word, I will treat Finn with the utmost respect. It may not even be him I seek."

"Regrettably, he visited London in May, ostensibly to stay with friends. Two days after his return, the manuscript appeared on my desk. No note, nothing to indicate from where, or whom, it had come. I have tried to assume the best but, of late, have lost my objectivity. Please be at my home at eleven tomorrow morning. One way or another, this needs to be dealt with, and I must get some sleep."

Thanking Kavanagh, Edward changed the subject by asking his guest about his ancestry, fascinated by tales of Viking invasions, ancient battles, clan chiefs and high kings. Donal knew his history and regaled Edward with tales, some possibly taller than others, well into the evening.

The following morning, at eleven prompt, Edward was ushered into a cavernous study in the Kavanagh's gracious residence. Donal rose to welcome the younger man and, after offering Edward a chair, resumed his seat behind the desk.

Edward had just made himself comfortable when there was a knock. A maid entered bearing a large silver tray on which stood three steaming cups of coffee and a plate of freshly baked oatmeal biscuits. On a smaller platter at the left of Donal's elbow, were three crystal tumblers each holding a generous measure of what Edward surmised to be whiskey.

Moments later there was another knock and the door opened to admit a slender man of average height. A shock of dark auburn hair, and a pair of watchful green eyes did little to soften an angular face. In fact, everything about the man seemed sharp, as though touching him would cut you.

His expression was belligerent, which interested Edward. Kavanagh's comments of the previous evening ran through his head, and intuition told him the marquis was correct, Finn Brennan was his man.

"Edward Lindsay, Finn Brennan. Finn, this is Edward Lindsay from London, he's staying with the Mackennas."

Edward studied Finn as they shook hands. The Irishman met his gaze with a rather cocksure one of his own. At Donal's invitation, they each took a cup of coffee and a biscuit, and sat down.

"You requested my attendance, cousin. How may I help?" Finn broke the silence which enveloped the three men while they sipped their drinks.

"By telling the truth. I have heard things, Finn, grave things; things which lead me to consider the possibility you might be involved." Donal steepled his fingers together and scrutinised his young relative.

"Me?" Finn's tone was the perfect blend of surprise and innocence. "What on earth do you suspect me of?"

"Murder."

The word hung in the air. Finn blanched, bounced out of his chair and, after jabbing a finger at Donal, spun to face Edward — his eyes narrowed to slits, his mouth an angry slash.

"Murder? *Me?* Surely, you jest? Oh, wait… is *that* why you came to Dublin? I am honoured, and there was I thinking you were simply doing your duty as guardian to the delightful Justina," he sneered.

Finn's mention of Justina sent ice down Edward's spine, but he replied pleasantly. "I *am* here as guardian to my sister. It was sheer coincidence that the idiot who decided to murder a peer of the realm chose to do so, immediately prior to our visit."

"So, of course, without any evidence, you assumed it *had* to be an Irishman. Then sought to inveigle your way into the good graces of this community, interrogating our friends, in the hope someone would confess to *murder*? You are addled."

"Our investigation led us to this conclusion, we did not *assume* anything. Moreover, Mr Brennan, this is not my first visit to Dublin," Edward countered, mildly, "I have no need to *inveigle* myself into anyone's graces. Save your cousin, I have known all in this neighbourhood for over twenty years. Neither have I interrogated anyone..." he paused and gave a grim smile, "... yet."

Donal intervened before Finn could respond, aware his cousin had a tendency to lose his temper and speak without thinking.

"Finn, you were in London in May. You knew how devastated I was, we all were, about the robbery, and loss of the manuscript. You made no mention either of the well-being of your friends, or what you did while visiting. Upon your return, earlier than expected I might add, my manuscript miraculously appears on my desk." Donal ticked the list off on his fingers.

"Pure chance," Finn barked.

"In that case you will not mind me asking a few questions?" Edward interjected, without rancour. Trained to read even the smallest signals, he knew Finn was guilty, but he was only there to garner information.

He explained as much, adding, "I no more want to accuse an innocent man, than excuse a guilty one, and you know I have no jurisdiction here. My mission is to uncover the truth, the rest is up to the magistrates in London."

Finn, glanced at Donal, and dropped back into his seat.
"I have nothing to hide. Ask away."

CHAPTER 9

*E*dward spent the next hour asking Finn numerous questions. Some seemed irrelevant, others incisive, and Edward was relentless, subtly extracting even the most minor detail.

Finn continued to deny any involvement, but Edward was satisfied it was he who committed both crimes. Some of Finn's answers led Edward to suspect he had acted under orders, astute enough to accept the former would not betray who that was.

"Thank you, Mr Brennan, that will be all." Edward had not taken any notes and maintained a polite manner throughout. He stood to take his leave, adding his appreciation to Donal for orchestrating this interview. His hand was on the doorknob when he turned and looked steadily at Finn.

"Whatever your assertions, I know you did this. I was already half-convinced following an earlier discussion. Your behaviour and responses during this last hour have merely compounded my belief. That said, you know I can do nothing; there is no concrete evidence and, on its own, my supposition is insufficient.

"I shall report my findings. Any further decision is up to my superiors. It would behove you not to do anything stupid while I await their instructions. If anything untoward befalls Lord Downe, or you are possessed with an unfortunate urge to use my sister as leverage, I will not be so… understanding, and retribution will be swift." He held Finn's gaze until the man inclined his head in acknowledgement.

Bowing to Donal, Edward left the room, only to pop back in seconds later, and with a wicked grin remarked, "Then again, who knows what might happen while guilt is being established. People disappear all the time." Without waiting for a reply, he departed, leaving Donal and Finn to figure out a solution they could live with.

Hungry, Edward treated himself to a pie from one of the street vendors and munched it while he walked back to Upper Mount Street. He was mulling over the discussion at Downe House when a voice from behind him, arrested his steps.

"Well, as I live and breathe, 'tis the elusive Mr Lindsay. I was beginning to think you'd run away again."

Edward spun on his heel to watch Aidan approach, and gave an apologetic smile. "I beg your forgiveness for my absence. I have been on the trail of a killer. It was rather more time-consuming and headache-inducing than I anticipated, but 'tis done." Relief ringing in his voice.

"Does this mean you are able to tell me what is going on?"

Edward considered Aidan's request. Without naming names, he could share some of what he had uncovered.

"Let us find a seat and I will recount what I can."

They were within minutes of the park where they had first met all those years ago. Edward glanced at Aidan who nodded slowly — it seemed oddly appropriate. By tacit agreement they made their way to the same bench, chatting about this and that. Once they were seated, and after gathering his thoughts, Edward provided Aidan with an abridged version of the case.

"You are convinced 'tis one of our own committed this murder?" Aidan asked when Edward concluded.

"Unfortunately, yes.

"Is your discovery cause for celebration?"

"In truth, I experienced no satisfaction in exposing the culprit. He has not confessed, nor do I expect he will. The death of Ravensgarth, while regrettable, has left many people, not least his wife and children, better off. He was a reprehensible man, whose only enjoyment in life was taking from others. Murder is a crime, it should be punished, but they have to catch the perpetrator first."

"I thought you had him?"

"I cannot prove it. It will take considerable time for my letter to reach London, and for a response — either written, or in the form of Lucas and his men — to reach me. What happens in the meantime is out of my hands."

A slow smile spread across Aidan's face. "You have given him a chance?"

"I will pretend I did not hear that. My loyalty is to the crown and the laws of England. I have done all I can."

"Do I know the suspect?"

"Probably, and because of this I will not name him. It protects you."

Aidan slid his palm under Edward's, interweaving their fingers. Edward stared at their joined hands, his heart aching at the sight. Their time together was coming to an end. He lifted his head, and his eyes searched Aidan's. *God, they were so blue, like a sun-kissed lake.* Ignoring how quixotic it sounded — they were his thoughts.

"What now?" Edward asked, feeling Aidan's fingers tighten around his.

"We seize every moment."

"I like your thinking."

"I might suggest we take a trip, but..."

"I would love to, when?" Edward interrupted, not allowing Aidan to talk himself out of it. "I shall send my letter and will need to await their reply. I expect it will take a fortnight or so. Justina is fine, Agatha will keep an eye on her." The idea of time alone with Aidan was irresistible.

A quick glance to ensure no one else was about, Aidan tilted his head, and their lips met in a leisurely kiss. Edward swore time slowed as heat coursed through him and blood rushed to that most inconvenient part of his body. Aidan's hand slid up his leg, thumb massaging the sensitive skin at the top of his thigh.

Edward bit back a groan. *Dammit they were in a public park*, although quite frankly, right then, he didn't care. Shuffling in his seat, he skimmed his hand over Aidan's jaw, and along under his ear to cup the back of his neck, stroking over sun-warmed skin.

Their kiss deepened and — if not for a flock of sparrows alighting in branches above them, whereupon they gave vent to a very noisy song — it is likely the two men would have let their ardour sweep them away.

Breathing heavily, Aidan broke their kiss and rested his forehead against Edward's. They were so close their eyelashes almost touched. Not for the first time, and doubtfully the last, Edward wished they could be open and honest about their relationship, while acknowledging it was a futile wish.

He understood why society feared anyone they deemed

different. London was brim-full of people from all walks of life, and he often overheard derogatory remarks about those arriving from foreign climes. To Edward, they were just people, yes, they might look a little unusual, but they were still just people.

In the same way they had no choice about how they looked, he had no choice about how he felt. To be considered deviant or an abomination because of something over which you had no control was difficult to come to terms with. Only Serena and Jonathon, and a handful of his most trusted friends knew.

"Liam has a cottage south of here. We often visited when I was younger. Perhaps he would be amenable to our staying there?"

"Sounds like a capital idea. I advise caution, however. I will let it be known I am travelling north and depart a day or so after you. My family have business interests about a day's ride from Dublin, and it has become my habit to check on them sporadically."

It didn't take them long to fine-tune the details and, as they strolled out of the park, Edward realised he felt genuinely happy.

CHAPTER 10

𝓛iam, although a little confused as to why Edward wanted to take a holiday alone, was glad to grant him the use of the cottage for as long as he wanted. He accepted his nephew's explanation he would benefit from a little peace and quiet after several weeks of intensive investigation.

Luggage, including a mountain of supplies was packed and sent on ahead with two staff — a maid and a footman — who would prepare the cottage for Edward's arrival.

The night before Edward was due to leave, he accompanied Justina to a ball. Although in recent years, it had become customary for the elite of Dublin to spend some of the Season in London, this year many chose not to, extolling the slower pace of summer at home.

There were plenty of balls, garden parties and picnics, but they were understated and less frequent. Yet another reason why Justina loved Dublin; she was not one for parties, preferring the quiet of green spaces to ballrooms.

This, however, was the first ball organised since their arrival, and probably the last major event of the Season, so everyone who was anyone would be attending.

Held at the home of the Duke and Duchess of Walkworth, the evening began splendidly. The house was full of light and colour and music. People mingled to a backdrop of laughter, chatter, and the clink of crystal. Alastar whisked Justina onto the dance floor, his expression when he saw her in a gown of palest turquoise, left none in any doubt of his affection.

Edward hoped to see Aidan during the evening, but as the clock ticked towards eleven, had yet to spot him. He was engaged in an interesting discussion with a small group of men, when they were distracted by a flurry of movement at the top of the short flight of stairs, which guests descended after greeting their hosts.

A sort of muted cheer went up, causing those below to pause and look up. Intrigued, Edward folded his arms and leant against a slender pillar at the edge of the ballroom

Lord Walkworth stepped to the ornate balustrade and raised his hand. The silence was immediate.

"Good evening, everyone. I hope you are enjoying yourselves. We have just heard some exciting news, which I begged to impart." A light chuckle rippled through the room; as though a duke would ever be denied. "It is my honour and delight to announce the betrothal of Miss Fionnuala Easby, daughter of Viscount Hazelmere to Viscount Bradhurst, eldest son of the Earl of Middleham." He ushered a clutch of people forward, but Edward did not need to hear anymore or be witness to their joy.

Viscount Bradhurst was Aidan.

. . .

Frozen with shock, Edward tried to make his brain function. His stomach roiled.

He had to get out.

Now.

How could Aidan have kept this from him? After all their plans. Surely, at some point in the last few days he might have had the decency to mention something so life changing.

Edward closed his eyes against the rush of emotions; hurt, anger, sorrow, and gut-wrenching disappointment. It was like watching his life on repeat.

Two years ago, in almost mirrored circumstances, he had heard the Earl of Middleham announce Aidan's betrothal to Orla. He felt a hand take his and, glancing down, saw Justina.

"Come with me," she exhorted. Blindly, Edward followed her, as she pulled him towards the huge French doors leading outside. At the last minute he turned and looked up, straight into Aidan's tortured gaze.

Their eyes clashed, and Edward was unable to tear his away. Aidan raised his hand as though petitioning him to stay, but Edward had not the strength. He had always known their time was ephemeral, but he never expected it to end in so brutal a manner.

"You can leave through the garden." Justina's words penetrated the fog in his head. "There is a gate to the right of the terrace. This way..." she tugged him with her and a moment later they were at an arched wooden gate nestled in the high stone wall.

"Justina...?" Edward tried, in vain, to make his mouth form the question.

"Edward, I know what you feel for Aidan. 'Tis the same as

I feel for Alastar, and if he was snatched away from me it would seem as though part of my soul had been severed. This must be killing you."

Edward gaped at his sister. "How... when... did... I thought you..." he shut up.

"I remember how you were two years ago. My wonderful, happy, cheerful, nothing got you down, brother changed overnight. You withdrew, you barely spoke. It was the same night Aidan's betrothal to Orla was announced. You left Dublin as soon as you could secure passage to London and, although little by little you began to shed the black cloud hanging over you, you were never quite the same. Until a month ago. You must deem me an insensitive dimwit indeed if you think I do not notice these things. Now go, I will inform our hosts you are unwell and left quietly so as not to interrupt the celebrations."

"Justina..." for the life of him Edward could not come up with anything else to say.

"Go. I shall see you on the morrow."

"I love you, sister-mine," he managed, dropping a kiss on her shining hair.

"I love you too." She squeezed his hand and unlatched the gate. Edward slipped through and, in seconds was enveloped into the darkness. Justina secured the gate, and stood for a moment, her fingers clutching the cool iron of the handle. Her heart was sore for her brother; Edward did not deserve this. Determined to get to the bottom of Aidan's duplicity, she marched back into the ballroom.

Edward hurried through the gloom and shortly thereafter was home. The house was blessedly quiet, the rest of the family were either still at the ball or in bed. Going into the library, he poured himself a generous measure of Brandy, and then stood by the windows overlooking the garden.

Gulping the spirit, he forced the evening out of his mind. It was done, over. A week or two alone with Aidan would only make their inevitable parting worse. It was better this way. He was a fool ever to think otherwise.

Tossing back the last of his drink, and taking a candle to light his way, Edward left the library. His long stride had him up the stairs and into his bedchamber in seconds. Placing the candle beside the bed, he stripped out of his evening attire, and shrugged into a pair of tan buckskins, a soft cotton shirt and plain waistcoat. He grabbed the jacket he wore when traipsing the bars of Dublin and, lastly, pulled on his boots.

Sitting at the escritoire, he penned a short note to his aunt and uncle saying he'd decided to travel to the cottage overnight because it was cooler; then another to Justina, thanking her. After folding and sealing them, Edward picked up his small travelling bag, blew out the candle, and hurried downstairs, placing both notes on the platter in the entrance hall.

Leaving by the back door, he went across the mews to the stable. Saddling the horse, Liam had loaned him for the duration of his stay in Dublin, Edward was soon trotting out of the city, guided by the moonlight.

CHAPTER 11

*W*hile Edward was preparing to ride south, Justina was seeking Aidan. Her fury at what she considered to be the betrayal of her brother, burned like bile in her throat and she was contemplating how many times she could feasibly punch Aidan before anyone stepped in.

It took some doing but, with Alastar in tow — making it seem as though the couple were hunting for a secluded corner — eventually, she tracked down Aidan. He was alone in a room at the far end of an unlit corridor, and an odd place for a newly affianced man to be hiding.

"Alastar, please ensure no one comes in." She brushed her lips to those of her suitor. Grinning, he agreed, murmuring words to the effect of, 'kiss me like that and I will do anything for you,' making her smile and kiss him again. "I shall only be a moment."

She crept in and closed the door with a quiet click. Aidan did not move. He was sitting, elbows on his knees, his hands hanging loosely between his legs, the picture of dejection.

"I came to offer you my congratulations, my lord," Justina's words were laden with sarcasm.

Aidan raised his head.

Her chest tightened at the devastation on his face, and she gentled her tones. "Or should I make that my condolences?" She sank onto the chair next to his and reached for his hand. "Aidan why do you let them do this?"

Startled, Aidan searched her face, nodding in acceptance that somehow Justina knew yet did not recoil. "They are my parents," he said flatly, and Justina knew it was not an excuse, merely a statement of fact. Among the peerage, alliances were formed through marriage, their children's wishes immaterial.

"After Orla I hoped..." she trailed off, unwilling to upbraid a man already wretched.

"As did I." The words sounded forced.

"Why did you not warn Edward?"

"I had no chance. The whole thing was presented to me as a *fait accompli* this evening not an hour before we left home. The agreement between my father and Lord Hazelmere is binding. Moreover, I do not know how I expected to escape marriage. I am the oldest son, the heir. My birth, my life is arranged to extend the line."

Justina observed Aidan in the flickering candlelight. "Do you love my brother?"

"If you are asking me that question, you know I do. We were supposed to go away..." he paused and shook his head. "God, I need a drink."

"Well, that won't help matters," she remonstrated. "Edward has gone. I expect he is halfway to the cottage by now." Aidan twisted to face her. She patted his knee. "I just thought you should know. What you do with the information is your decision." She smiled, then pinned him with a steely glare. "Mind, but if you hurt my brother again, I will make your life more of a living hell than it is now."

Justina stood, and pressed a quick kiss to Aidan's cheek. "Don't waste your life, Aidan, there is always a way. The only question is, do you live the lie or follow your heart?"

Then she was gone in a whisper of silks, the murmur of voices fading as she and Alastar disappeared down the corridor.

Aidan sat for a long time ruminating over Justina's words. She was right. While marriage to Fionnuala would not be arduous, he was not being fair to her. He doubted he would have any desire to perform his husbandly duties, the very idea made him nauseous. Thus, the whole point of their nuptials was void. He *had* to extricate himself from this farce, but how?

Fionnuala was a lovely girl, she would make anyone a wonderful wife, just not him. He ruminated over this for a while, then a thought occurred to him. Connor — his brother, at just two years younger would be admirable, should the two patriarchs agree. It was time he took control of his fate.

Three hours, two irate families, one very understanding and astute young lady — much to Aidan's surprise — and an ecstatic brother later, Aidan was riding out of Dublin as though the hounds of hell were after him.

His parents had been shocked, horrified, and speechless when he explained why he could not continue with the betrothal, and that he was prepared to relinquish his title to Connor. This meant, legalities aside, the announcement did not need to be retracted or amended, no one lost face, and there was a decent likelihood of an heir.

It transpired Fionnuala and Connor knew and liked each other; they shared the same extended group of friends and had enjoyed more than the occasional dance together. Hopefully, even so modest a connection would be enough on which to build a life. It was already more than most marriages among the nobility began with, and definitely more than Aidan could offer.

Whatever happened, Aidan knew he could not marry. Edward was right, it was unfair to the lady he wed. It would only ever be a marriage in name — no children, no heir. Bachelorhood was his path and as he rode, Aidan felt a burden, one he did not realise he carried, roll off his shoulders. He felt free. With a loud whoop of unadulterated joy, which disturbed a nearby flock of sheep, Aidan hoped he wasn't too late.

Dawn was just breaking when Aidan reached the cottage, and despite the early hour, he was not the only one awake. After stabling his horse, he noticed the back door was wide open. He stuck his head through and called a soft hello. No response. Continuing on into the main house, he glanced around, all was quiet. No sound of the staff bustling about. So why was the door open?

Going back outside, he scanned his surrounds. He heard a muffled splash… the beach.

Curious now, he retraced his steps, and dropped his bag

on the floor just inside the kitchen. Pulling the back door closed, he strode along the grassy path to the shore. The sun was beginning its slow climb across a pale blue sky, the fiery orb reflecting on the sea like liquid gold.

As though by design, a tall figure rose from the sparkling waves. His powerful physique, silhouetted by the radiant sunlight, made Aidan's heart lurch and his breathing quicken.

Edward!

Edward had not slept. His precipitous arrival had thrown the staff into a mild panic, but he assured them he just needed his bed. Slumber eluded him. The evening kept replaying through his head. The joy of the guests, the happiness of the family, and Aidan's face.

Part of him, his idealistic side, wished he had stayed to soothe his — what was he? — not even a lover, but so much more than a friend. His practical side accepting that although Aidan was his soulmate... his *anamchara*, the Gaelic resounding through him like a heartbeat... he was lost to him forever.

After tossing and turning until the darkness of the room began to change, the grey light of the new day filtering through the unshuttered window, Edward got up. He looked out over the bay; the water called to him. He had learnt to swim here. Being a pastime in which he could rarely indulge, he wanted to take full advantage while at the cottage. Also, he hoped the exercise would be beneficial. If nothing else, it ought to exhaust him enough that he might get some sleep.

He pulled a banyan over his nightshirt and was on the narrow beach in minutes. The air was crisp so early in the morning, the sun just peeking over the horizon. He was the only person abroad. Perfection.

Dropping his clothes on the grass at the edge of the beach, Edward walked cautiously into the sea, shivering a little as the chill water rippled across his warm skin. When he was thigh deep, he plunged in and swam until his arms began to ache. Turning onto his back, the waves lapping around his body, he floated for a while, catching his breath.

As the sun rose, he flipped over and struck out for the shore.

His fingers touched sand. He brought his legs under him and pushed himself upright, water cascading off his body.

He spied a figure on the beach.

Was that Aidan?

The figure moved.

Edward could see clothes being flung, smothering a laugh when, hopping in his haste to remove his boots, the visitor all but fell flat on his backside.

The man, tanned, muscular, and wickedly handsome, splashed towards him. Edward's heart thudded. Even knowing this was highly irregular, he had no mind to call a halt, praising every God in the existence of the world that they were miles from civilisation.

Aidan had come... *for him*!

Edward opened his mouth but, as seemed to be a habit of late, words stuck in his throat. Aidan reached him, and hesitated.

They stared, drinking each other in.

Here, in the quiet of the morning, it was the first time either had seen the other completely naked. The frissons prickling over sun-brushed skin nothing to do with the cool breeze.

Edward heard himself gulp. "Aidan..." he managed, little more than a croaking husk.

"Edward, *mo chroí*, my heart."

It was enough — later they would talk — now they came together in an almost frenzied tangle of limbs, crashing into the water. Hands and lips, searching, learning, tasting... loving.

EPILOGUE

DUBLIN ~ SEPTEMBER 1817

*T*he three-masted merchant vessel slid out of *Calafort Átha Cliath*. Four men on deck waved to the crowd, gathered to farewell them. A stiffening breeze lifted the sails and soon the boat was out of the harbour, scudding across the water.

Major Lucas Withers and Lord Mayhew wandered away, chatting about this and that. The other two stood motionless watching the land shrink slowly from view.

An eventful summer, and one which might well have been remembered for all the wrong reasons — murder, theft, heartache and sadness — had managed to redeem itself.

Justina and Alastar were betrothed, the couple choosing December and London for their wedding.

Serena and Jonathon Mayhew had travelled to Dublin with Lucas Withers after receiving letters from Justina and Edward respectively. None was sure what they would find, relieved to discover all was well.

Serena, invited to stay with Justina and the Mackennas, would return to London with the rest of the wedding entourage.

Lucas concurred with Edward's findings, but of Finn Brennan, there was no sign. He had vanished as though he had never existed. His actions, however laudable, had resulted in his life being consigned to the fringes — and, hard though it would be, was better than being forfeit. That he may have been carrying out orders was never established.

Edward and Aidan had talked... *a lot.* Theirs was perhaps a harder road than Finn's. Despite his crimes, the latter could live under an assumed name, marry, have children, take a job. Constrained by the rule of law, Edward and Aidan could never acknowledge their love publicly — extreme discretion was now the tenet by which they must abide.

Not that any of this swayed their decision. They had come up with a plan. One which needed the finer points ironing out, but it was a start — further, and unwittingly, aided by Lucas Withers. Impressed by what he saw of Aidan, and aware how valuable a Dublin connection might prove, Lucas offered him a role within his organisation.

Turning his head slightly, Edward studied Aidan. His lover's — oh, how he adored that word — face bore no expression. Edward could not conceive how difficult this must be. To leave the only home you have ever known, your family, your friends. He felt a familiar ache swell in his chest.

"There is still time, if you think this is a mistake," he said quietly.

Aidan met Edward's troubled gaze, and his countenance softened. "'Tis just an adjustment is all. I..."

"I know we have talked about this, but Dublin is your home and 'tis so beautiful..." Edward interrupted, then, typically, ran out of words.

"*Mo ghrá.*" The lilting endearment, tangible as a caress, made Edward tingle. "My home is with you. Yes, I shall miss Dublin but without you, 'tis mere bricks and mortar. You are my life, my heart, my soul. It has taken us six years to get here and, although we thought it would remain naught but a fantasy, our love has been very much worth the wait." His cheeks reddening a little at how poetic he sounded.

They grinned at each other, unrestrained beams of pure happiness.

Finally!

Under a sky as blue as Aidan's eyes, with the cry of the seagulls wheeling overhead, and the rhythmic slap of the waves against the hull of the ship echoing his heartbeat, Edward did the unthinkable. He kissed Aidan; his gesture more profound than any words.

Against all odds, that which was unimaginable, inconceivable and unattainable — in fact, a love impossible — was no longer a dream, but a reality they could share for a lifetime.

EXCERPT FROM RESCUING HER KNIGHT

PROLOGUE - EASBY HALL 1798

*I*t was an idyllic, late summer's afternoon. Here and there, white fluffy clouds punctuated the dazzlingly blue sky. The gentle fragrance of honeysuckle drifted on the balmy air, along with the warble of birdsong and the buzz of lazy insects. From beyond the formal gardens echoed the sound of children playing.

Several adults sat in a loose circle on the stone flagged terrace. The women sipped cool lemonade; the men opting for wine or perhaps a brandy. Something about the relaxed poses of the four couples suggested an abiding friendship; a notion confirmed by their topics of conversation — had anyone been listening.

Unusually in this era, although their marriages had been arranged, each man was devoted to his wife — an affection reciprocated. Taking every opportunity to get together, even if only briefly, their easy camaraderie had led to their offspring being similarly disposed to each other. Despite a thirteen-year age gap between oldest and youngest, and although not all were bound by blood, the children were closer than many siblings.

. . .

The tranquil scene was shattered by a high-pitched shriek and, as one, the adults rose to their feet to hurry in the direction of the sound. The screams continued unabated and when the first parent rounded the hedge delineating the formal gardens and the orchards, he was met by a sight which made him question whether a massacre had occurred.

A little girl, covered in blood, was being tended to by an older boy also duly spattered. The other children were hovering, their mouths agape.

"Please stop wriggling, Kitty. I know it hurts but I need to stop the bleeding." Using his kerchief, the boy was trying, desperately, to staunch the blood welling from the child's leg.

"Mama, I want Mama." Kitty sobbed, her tears clearing two tracks down grubby cheeks.

"Mama is coming," the adult spoke from above them, prompting the boy to swing his gaze upward, relief painting his features and his voice.

"*Papa*. Please help. We were running, and Kitty tripped, and…" he trailed off. It was apparent what had happened. "There is so much blood." For all his pluck, his face had taken on a slightly green tinge.

"Good lad. Here, let me carry her. Come on, poppet. Let's get you indoors and see to your knee." Carefully, the gentleman scooped Kitty into his arms,

"**Adam**," Hiccuping, Kitty reached out a chubby hand to the boy. He grasped it, squeezing her fingers gently.

"Papa will look after you." Adam said with a child's unwavering faith their parents' abilities to fix everything.

By this time, the remaining adults had arrived, gathering their respective children, and giving them a quick once over to ensure no one else was hurt.

"We are all fine," Adam volunteered. "Just Kitty."

Over the heads of the youngsters, the adults shared a collective grin. It was always 'just Kitty'. The child seemed to attract mishaps. If it wasn't falling flat on her face, it was cutting herself on a sheet of paper, or stabbing herself with a quill, or dropping something — usually breakable and usually onto one of her feet.

Six-year-old, Katherine de Wilton or, as everyone called her, Kitty, was a walking disaster. It never bothered her. She picked herself up or righted whatever she had knocked over and carried on. She was unfailingly cheerful, even in the face of adversity, which made this accident all the more serious.

Kitty rarely cried. When she broke her arm the previous winter after taking an awkward tumble while learning to ice skate, she didn't cry. When she was given the news about her grandfather's death, she was more concerned about her mama being sad. The only other time any of them present could recall seeing her weep was when one of the dogs died.

"Mama," her screams had diminished to a forlorn wail as her mother, Frederica de Wilton, Lady Grafton, came forward.

"I'm here, precious, no need for such a rumpus. Uncle Reginald will take you inside." Frederica stroked damp curls out of her daughter's face. "You *do* get into some scrapes."

Kitty heaved a resigned sigh. "Mama, I am only six. Things are *bound* to happen when you're six." Her long-suffering tone indicating to her listeners this ought to be blindingly obvious. "Where's Adam?"

"I'm here, Kitty." The youth's face appeared in her line of vision.

"Thank you. You are my knight in shining armour." She bestowed on him a watery smile.

Thirteen-year-old Adam blushed to the roots of his dark brown hair. "No, I'm not," he mumbled.

The other children cheered with delight when they heard

this. "Yes, you are. Our knight. Adam Marchmain, Knight of the Garden." They began to march in front of the adults, repeating their declaration as a nonsensical ditty. Then before anyone could stop them, ran off to get up to more mischief.

Adam lingered, keeping step with his father, unsure whether it was quite appropriate to play when one of their number was wounded. *Knights were supposed to attend to a damsel in distress, weren't they?* When they reached the terrace, his father, taking pity on him, bent his head and told his son to scoot.

"Go on, Adam. Kitty will be fine after a bath."

"Are you sure?"

"Yes but, if you are worried, come back in half an hour. You'll see, she will have all but forgotten she took a tumble."

"It is a nasty cut, Papa."

"I can see that, but I do not think she will lose her leg." Reginald Marchmain's tone was jovial. A comforting sign to Adam who knew when his father spoke like this, the situation was not dire.

"All right. Half an hour?"

Reginald nodded and Adam fled in search of the others.

Kitty was duly bathed, the water turning a lovely shade of brown as the mud and all manner of detritus was washed off. Clean, and in a fresh dress, she was conveyed to the library, where one of their number, David Wells, the Marquis of Clarence who had a little medical knowledge, inspected the injury. Adam was correct, it was nasty. A relatively long and jagged laceration under Kitty's knee.

"I think you ought to call for the doctor," he said, placidly. "It might need suturing.

"What does that mean, Uncle David?" Kitty was staring at her knee with gruesome avidity.

Frederica crouched by her daughter who was lying on the couch. "It means the doctor uses a needle and cotton to tie the edges of the cut together. Similar to how I sew."

Kitty's eyes widened, then she giggled. "Mama, you are silly. You cannot sew people. I am not a tapestry, or a doll."

"I am very much afraid, you can. Doctors do it all the time."

Kitty's courage drained away like the last of the bathwater. She shook her head. "No, no, no, no, no. That is not a good idea. Putting holes in a person's skin. I don't want to be sut… stut… sewn up. I will look like Betsy." Betsy was a very old and very well-loved doll; one Frederica had played with as a child. Betsy had been repaired numerous times and she was now more stitch than doll. Kitty took Betsy everywhere, even to bed.

"You will not look like Betsy…"

Kitty pinned her mother with a penetrating and uncannily adult stare.

"…well, perhaps a teeny tiny bit, but sweetheart, if the doctor thinks your leg needs stitching, you will need to be my brave girl and let him."

By now, Kitty was all for running away, but any movement made her leg bleed. Truth be told, she was feeling queasy and, reluctantly, submitted to her mother's tender care.

The doctor arrived and decreed the wound did indeed require several sutures. "It will keep bleeding if we do not," he explained to Kitty, who by now was decidedly averse to the whole idea.

"Come now, Kitty. It will only take a minute. If you let Doctor Arthurs treat your leg, I will ask Uncle Reginald whether you might have an ice." Frederica was past caring whether bribing her child was appropriate. Kitty was scared and rightly so. Suturing wounds was not for the faint hearted. If an ice persuaded her, it was worth it.

"I shall go and check forthwith," Reginald agreed and disappeared to speak to one of the maids out of Kitty's hearing.

Adam poked his head around the door. "How is Kitty?" he asked.

"Adam," Kitty's whimper had him scuttling over the carpet to her side.

"Does it hurt?"

"Yes, and the doctor wants to sew it." Panic laced her tones.

Adam dropped to his knees next to the sofa. "Only the most valiant of soldiers dare be sutured," he remarked, contemplatively. "They usually get a medal."

"I am only six. I doubt there is a medal for being a brave six-year-old."

"I'll wager there is." Hoping he was not about to be proved wrong, Adam lifted his head to scan the faces of the adults in the room — his mother, Kitty's parents, and the doctor. Ernest de Wilton, Kitty's father, understood immediately and nodding, left the room. Adam kept up a flow of chatter distracting Kitty, while the doctor prepared his instruments.

Reginald returned to inform Kitty a large bowl of chocolate ice was being prepared at this very moment

Dr Arthurs rinsed the needle in vinegar, then threaded it.

He shot a glance at Frederica who inclined her head and settled behind Kitty, wrapping the small girl in her arms.

"Kitty, this will be painful, but I will be as quick as possible. You need to be a..." he looked at Adam, "...valiant soldier."

Kitty's bottom lip wobbled.

Adam inched closer and took her hand.

"Please will you tell me a story, Adam?" her face was sheet white and, even though Adam was only thirteen, he could tell she was terrified.

"I don't know any stories," he hedged.

"Once upon a time..."

Adam stared at her, slightly confused. *Wasn't he supposed to be telling the story?*

"...that's how they start." Her hot little hand gripped his.

Grinning, Adam scoured his brain for a story, any story. It was a long time since he had bothered to listen to stories, they were for babies.

Dr Arthurs began. The instant the needle pierced Kitty's skin, she squealed, and two fat tears spilled over.

"B-b-b-b..."

"Once upon a time, in a land faraway there was a beautiful princess, whose name was Caterina." Adam rushed to interject. Kitty pressed her lips together and squeezed his fingers tightly in one hand, clutching her mother's arm in the other. "She had curly blonde hair, and green eyes."

"Ohhhh, 'tis me." Kitty exclaimed.

"One day, she was out riding her horse—"

"What was the horse's name," Kitty interrupted, her voice croaking when the doctor pulled the needle.

"Mmmm... Bluebell."

"I love bluebells," the little girl beamed at Adam

"I know. Do you want to hear the story or not?"

"Continue," she intoned imperiously, prompting her mother to smother a grin.

There was a loud hiss when the thread was drawn through.

Noticing Kitty's expression, Adam hurried on. "The princess was riding Bluebell through the woods and through the meadows. They rode for a long time until they came to the river which marked the border of her father's lands. The princess had never travelled beyond the boundary and wanted to explore. The river was deep and fast flowing. Bluebell hesitated at the water's edge, but the princess was too excited to recognise the danger and urged the mare on."

"Ohhhh, what happened?" Caught up in the story Kitty was becoming less aware of the needle's sting.

"Bluebell struggled to keep her footing. Realising they might be swept away, the princess panicked and screamed for help. Bluebell joined in, neighing loudly, and between them, they created a fair din.

"Suddenly, on the opposite bank, another horse appeared. A huge black stallion, ridden by a tall stranger. Before Caterina could repeat her plea, the stranger and his horse were in the river splashing towards her. The man grasped Bluebell's reins and led them out of the torrent. As soon as they reached the safety of the bank, the stranger dipped his head, and turned to ride away.

'Wait, kind sir. You saved my life, or at the very least prevented me from suffering a drenching. Such a brave act deserves a reward.' The princess cried.

'No reward is necessary. It is my pleasure and honour to rescue so beautiful a maiden.'

The princess blushed. "Thank you. I am in your debt.'

'Fair lady, there is no debt.' The rider bowed his head, and with a wave of his hand was gone. The end." Adam, who had no idea what to say next, finished abruptly.

"Is *that* it?" A disgruntled Kitty chimed in.

The doctor snipped the last suture.

"Knights rescue damsels in distress but always leave without giving their name. 'Tis in all the books. Anyway, Dr Arthurs has finished."

"What happens?" Kitty folded her arms and glowered.

"Don't be rude, Kitty. Adam has told a charming story and here is Uncle Reginald with your ice." Frederica chided.

"I will finish it another time," Adam vowed, rashly.

"Promise?"

"I promise."

Kitty's father, appeared carrying a cushion, on which lay a medal. In actuality it was an old but impressive-looking coin, which Reginald had procured for somewhere. With a flourish, he presented it to his small daughter, effectively diverting her.

For a while, the story was forgotten.

ABOUT THE AUTHOR

Rosie Chapel lives in Perth, Australia with her hubby and three furkids. When not writing, she loves catching up with friends, burying herself in a book (or three), discovering the wonders of Western Australia, or — and the best — a quiet evening at home with her husband, enjoying a glass of wine and a movie.

Website: www.rosiechapel.com

OTHER BOOKS BY ROSIE CHAPEL

<u>Historical Fiction</u>
The Hannah's Heirloom Sequence
The Pomegranate Tree - Book One
Echoes of Stone and Fire - Book Two
Embers of Destiny - Book Three
Etched in Starlight - Prequel
Hannah's Heirloom Trilogy - Compilation – e-book only

Prelude to Fate

<u>Regency Romances</u>
The Linen and Lace Series
Once Upon An Earl - Book One
To Unlock Her Heart - Book Two
Love on a Winter's Tide - Book Three
A Love Unquenchable - Book Four
A Hidden Rose - Book Five

The Daffodil Garden
The Unconventional Duchess
Rescuing Her Knight

His Fiery Hoyden
A Regency Duet
A Regency Christmas Double
Fate is Curious

A Christmas Prayer with Ashlee Shades

The Lady's Wager

Winning Emma

A Love Impossible

<u>Fairy Tale Romance</u>

Chasing Bluebells

<u>Contemporary Romances</u>

Of Ruins and Romance

All At Once It's You

Cobweb Dreams

Just One Step

His Heart's Second Sigh

HISTORICAL FICTION

The Pomegranate Tree

Hannah's Heirloom - Book One

Hoping to trace the origins of an ancient ruby clasp, a gift from her long dead grandmother, Hannah Wilson travels to the fortress of Masada with her best friend, Max. Strange dreams concerning a rebel ambush begin to haunt Hannah and following a tragic accident, she slips into the world of Ancient Masada.

A woman out of time, Hannah must rely on her instincts and her knowledge of what will befall this citadel to survive. Will she escape, or is she doomed to die along with hundreds of others as Masada falls – and what does any of this have to do with an ancient ruby clasp?

Echoes of Stone and Fire

Hannah's Heirloom - Book Two

Pompeii - a vibrant city lost in time following the AD79 eruption of Vesuvius. Now rediscovered, archaeologists yearn for an opportunity to uncover the town's past. Some things, however, are best left alone - revealing the secrets hidden beneath the stones could prove perilous. Hannah and Max are brought to Pompeii by a surprise invitation to join an excavation team who are trying to uncover the city's long history.

After entering an excavated house that bears a Hebrew inscription, Hannah's two worlds collide, and she falls back through time to ancient Pompeii. A place where her ancestor is a physician to gladiators engaged in mortal combat, where riotous mobs run amok and where a ghost from the past returns to haunt her.

Will Hannah and her loved ones manage to escape the devastation she knows is coming, before the town is engulfed in volcanic ash?

Will she ever find her way back to Max the love of her life, waiting not so patiently millennia away? Or will echoes be all that remain?

Embers of Destiny

Hannah's Heirloom - Book Three

AD80 - Hannah and Maxentius must embark on a new journey to Northern Britannia. This harsh frontier is far from the comforts of Rome and danger lurks where least expected; a garrison of soldiers, some unhappy with their isolated posting; local tribes, outwardly accepting of their Roman occupier, but who may still resent the seizure of their lands.

Millennia away, Hannah Vallier finds a familiar item while working in a museum near Hadrian's Wall. It is the pomegranate; carved by Maxentius on Masada. Before Hannah can discuss it with Max, disaster strikes! Believing her husband has been killed, Hannah retreats into the past, her soul melding with that of her ancestor, but with little idea of what they could face. Is the risk from the conquered tribes, or much closer to home?

As rebellion threatens to shatter a fragile peace, Hannah's heart whispers that just maybe Max isn't dead and that he is calling her home. Can she trust her heart, or will she remain caught out of time, her destiny floating away like embers on a breeze?

Etched in Starlight

Hannah's Heirloom - Prequel

Maxentius - a Roman soldier fresh from the battlefields of Armenia, arrives to take command of the military outpost of Masada, Herod's isolated citadel in the Judaean desert. A seemingly mundane posting after years of warfare, Maxentius finds it more challenging to maintain a focused garrison than to face the wrath of the Parthians across a disputed frontier.

Hannah - a young Hebrew physician spends her days dealing with injuries from street brawls, deprivation, disease and loss. As her beloved Jerusalem plunges into chaos; her brother — who belongs to a band of rebels determined to drive out their Roman occupiers — tells her of their plans to storm a desert fortress and steal the weapons stored there, persuading his reluctant sister to go with him.

Masada - following the ambush, Hannah finds and treats three badly wounded Roman soldiers. In the aftermath and against impossible odds, Hannah and Maxentius realise that they are more than healer and captive, their fate already etched in starlight.

Prelude to Fate

For Lucia, staring into the jaws of an horrific death, escape seems impossible.

Rufius Atellus, a veteran Roman soldier, is appalled when he recognises one of the victims about to be executed. Surely this is a ghastly mistake?

A ferocious she-wolf, anticipating a tasty meal, suddenly finds herself under a human's control.

In an unexpected twist, and as danger threatens, the lives of all three become inextricably entwined.

Was it chance brought them together in that theatre of bloodshed, or simply a prelude to fate?

Once Upon An Earl

Linen and Lace - Book One

When Fate saw fit to intervene in the life of Giles Trevallier, the very respectable Earl of Winchester, by dropping a female — soaked to the skin and with no memory of who she is or how she came to be there — literally at his feet, no one could have predicted the outcome.

While uncovering her identity, Giles realises he is falling hopelessly in love with his mystery guest, who unbeknownst to him, is succumbing to similar emotions; but, when the heart is involved, a thoughtless word or gesture can thwart even Fate's best-laid plans.

Faced with misunderstandings, whispers of scandal, secret documents and foreign agents, their chance at a happy ever after seems elusive, but fairy tales often happen when least expected, and love — however inconvenient — usually finds a way to conquer all.

To Unlock Her Heart

Linen and Lace - Book Two

Abused by a duke, and shunned by Society, relief seems at hand when Grace Aldeburgh is bequeathed a house in a small village, far from malicious gossips.

Once there, a tentative friendship blooms between Grace and Theo Elliott, the local doctor, who has already resolved to be the man to unlock her heart.

Just when happiness appears to be within her grasp, her erstwhile tormentor once again stalks Grace. After a failed kidnap attempt, the duke's quest culminates in an acrimonious confrontation, and the reason for his venal pursuit becomes agonisingly clear.

Love on a Winter's Tide

Linen and Lace - Book Three

Every day, Helena disappears into a world few acknowledge, helping the poor, downtrodden, and abused. A husband is the last thing she can be bothered with.

Busy managing his shipping line, Hugh Drummond sees no need for a wife, whose only joy is dancing and frivolity. If — and it was a huge if — he ever married, it would be to a woman as capable as he, not some giddy society Miss.

Then, Hugh meets Helena and despite their resolve, fate, it seems, has other ideas. As their attraction deepens however, treachery threatens to tear them apart. Will they uncover the perpetrator in time, or will their love be swept away, lost forever on a winter's tide?

A Love Unquenchable

Linen and Lace - Book Four

Jessica Drummond, a bright and cheerful young woman, rarely gives romance, let alone love, a thought. Long hours working in her brother's shipping office affords little chance of her ever meeting an eligible bachelor.

Duncan Barrington, veteran of the Napoleonic Wars, believes himself wounded in both body and soul. He has no intention of inflicting his demons on anyone, certainly not a beautiful and, in his opinion, irresponsible city lady.

One cold and snowy morning, the plight of a bedraggled puppy throws Jessica and Duncan together and, as a spark of something indefinable yet wholly unquenchable begins to burn, it is unclear who rescued whom.

A Hidden Rose

Linen and Lace - Book Five

After witnessing his mother's grief at the loss of his father, Nick Drummond resolved never to cause someone he loved such distress. Even the happiness of his siblings would not sway him – until he met Rose.

Rose Archer was almost content assisting her doctor father in a tiny fishing village in the north of Yorkshire. To experience the world beyond, a tantalising dream – until she met Nick.

Unexpectedly, the impossible becomes possible, and the renounced – desired above all things, but the shipwreck that brought them together, may yet tear them apart. Will Nick learn to trust his heart, or will his love for Rose remain forever hidden

The Daffodil Garden

Horrifically scarred during the war, William Harcourt - Marquis of Blackthorne - prefers to spend his days in the quiet of his daffodil garden; plants do not pity, turn away, or judge.

Lucy Truscott, whose life is far removed from that of the *ton*, has no idea that by saving the life of a young woman, to whom she bears an uncanny resemblance, her own will be placed in mortal danger.

A chance encounter leads to something more. William begins to trust that Lucy sees the man beneath the scars, while Lucy is persuaded that love might actually transcend status.

Unfortunately, before their courtship has really begun, someone has every intention of ending it - permanently.

The Unconventional Duchess

Refusing to suffer the humiliation of her husband flaunting his mistress at Society events, the newly married Duchess of

Wallingstead, Ella Lennox, takes control of her life. She leaves London for the family's country seat in remote Yorkshire.

A woman alone, Ella spends the next four years turning a cold, grim house into a home, and transforming the fortunes of the estate. Not afraid of hard work, she soon earns the respect of those around her with her determination and unconventional attitude.

Out of the blue, the duke arrives. Resigned to another arduous visit, Ella is stunned when it seems he is attempting to court her.

Impossible!

Could her dream of a happy marriage be about to come true?

Everything hangs on a snowstorm, a herd of cows and an uninvited guest!

Rescuing Her Knight

The de Wiltons - Book One

A story, invented to keep a little girl distracted, marks the beginning of another tale. One destined to remain unfinished for nearly twenty years.

Against her better judgement, Kitty de Wilton is persuaded to help Adam Marchmain banish his demons. This requires a subterfuge which, if discovered, might shatter more than the bonds of friendship forged two decades previously.

To Kitty, determined to break through the shield Adam has erected, the risk is worth it.

To see his smile and hear his laughter.

To rescue the knight of her childhood.

Just when a fairy tale ending is within her grasp, Kitty is threatened by the man who murdered her husband. In a cruel twist the tables are turned, and Kitty is the one who needs rescuing.

His Fiery Hoyden

A Novella

Livvy has no respect for the nobility; they let her down when she most needed them. Why should she accede to their demands now?

Philip, Lord Harrington, is stunned to discover the young heir to the dukedom lives a stone's throw away in a ramshackle cottage, and resolves to restore the child to his birthright.

They meet in a clash of wills, but just when it seems Livvy might surrender, the victory Philip desires, may not taste all that sweet.

A Regency Duet

Luck be a Pirate

Luck wasn't something retired pirate Kennet Alexson believed in – good or bad. However, even he had to concede that landing a job at Trentams shipyard, and meeting Lynette Collins, was more than coincidence.

Fortune it seemed, was smiling on him for once.

As Kennet adjusts to life on dry land, his friendship with Lynette deepens into something far more enduring, and what once seemed elusive now becomes possible.

Unfortunately, fate has other plans, and Kennet's good luck is about to run out.

The Highwayman's Kiss

Surrendered Hearts – Book One

Nothing exciting had ever happened to Juliette St Clair. Her days were spent assisting her father or calling on friends, wandering art galleries, taking constitutionals or, and more preferably, escaping into her books. Her evenings her evenings — an endless round of balls, where she preferred to remain invisible.

Until the day she was robbed by a highwayman.

A Regency Christmas Double

Heart Rescued

Four years since Jasper lost the woman he was hoping to marry. Four years since he closed his heart and withdrew from Society. He has no idea his reclusive existence is about to be shattered.

Enter his sister's best friend, Harriet, a flame haired beauty, who needs his help.

Reluctantly he agrees and as they spend time together, it is clear their feelings run deep. Although Harriet affects Jasper in a way no woman ever has, he believes her to be out of his league ~ but it's Christmas and she might just be the one to melt his frozen heart

Catch a Snowflake

Romance often blossoms in the most unlikely of places - but in a ward full of wounded soldiers - surely not?

When Lucas Withers comes face to face with Jemima Parsons - a young woman who blames him for her brother's injury - falling in love is the last thing on their minds. What neither of them anticipated, was the magic of snowflakes.

Fate is Curious

A Novella

Happily, ever after? No such thing! Bereft, following her beloved husband's sudden death, Lady Charlotte Sherbrooke has lost her belief in such romantic nonsense.

Successful shipping merchant, Zacharie Romain, is no stranger to loss; his business can be hazardous. Moreover, his wife died in childbirth and even though it happened a decade ago, he has no mind to expose himself to such sorrow again.

They meet in less than joyful circumstances but, as the year turns and grief diminishes, the woes of a small boy become the catalyst for something wholly unexpected. Can Charlotte and Zacharie trust what Fate has in store or will past heartbreak prevent them from taking a chance on love?

A Christmas Prayer

with Ashlee Shades

A Short Story

An entreaty from a frightened child.

Orphaned and only nine, Caroline Thorne has to grow up before her time. She is doing everything she can to keep what is left of her family together and out of the workhouse but is terrified her prayers are not being heard. Or maybe they are...

A petition from a woman desperate for a family.

A chance meeting with three orphaned siblings, tugs at Elizabeth Barrington's heart strings. Thus far, she and her husband have not been blessed with children and, as Christmas approaches, a plan begins to form - one which might just be the answer to her prayers.

Two Christmas prayers, as different as they are the same.

Will they hear and, more importantly, heed the answer?

The Lady's Wager

Surrendered Hearts- Book Two

A Novelette

Ged Mowbray will do anything to avoid being married off to the suitable prospects his parents insist on parading in front of him.

Melissa Bouchard is under no illusion her sizeable dowry is the attraction to suitors, not her.

An overheard conversation leads to an offer too good to refuse, but what happens when a lady's wager, becomes a gamble on the happily ever after, you did not even realise you wanted?

Winning Emma

Surrendered Hearts - Book Three

A Novelette

Randolph Craythorpe — earl, covert operative, and occasional highwayman — believed his dalliance with Lady Felicity Hartwich would lead to marriage. It did, but not to him! The arrival of an unwelcome guest, however, provides the perfect opportunity to indulge in a little retaliation.

Emma Newbury accompanies her cousin, Lady Charity Anscombe, to London for the Christmas season. Once there, she comes face to face with the three men who witnessed the humiliating aftermath of her father's disgrace — one of whom, to her irritation, has taken up residence in her dreams.

Their infrequent encounters only serve to confuse but, while winter tightens its grip on the city, what was inconceivable becomes the one thing for which they both yearn, yet bound by Society's rules, cannot admit.

As the snow falls, Randolph begins to understand that to win Emma, he will have to surrender.

FAIRY TALE ROMANCE

Chasing Bluebells

A Novella

Once upon a time, somewhere in France, there was a man whose reckless obsession led him down a dark path. One which, ultimately, cost him his life.

That ought to have been the end of it. Regrettably, as is so often the case, those who least deserve it, suffer for the actions of others.

A decade after being sent away, Sebastien Daviau returns to the little village where everything began, hoping to lay the ghosts of his childhood to rest, studiously ignoring the possibility, he might run into Charlotte de Montbeliard.

As luck would have it, Charlotte is the one who runs into him... well his horse. Although the encounter leaves a lasting impression, neither recognises the other.

A name revealed causes a freak accident, catapulting Sebastien's past into his present, and bringing him face to face with a man whose reputation would intimidate the most ardent of suitors.

Can whatever is blossoming between Charlotte and Sebastien survive the challenge imposed, or is their happily ever after about to fade as quickly as the bluebells they loved to chase?

❖

Of Ruins and Romance

Kassandra Winters has intrigued Gabriel St Germain since he accidentally knocked her flying outside her university professor's office. Her face haunts his dreams, yet he never expected to see her again. So, he is surprised when she appears, as though destined to do so, in the middle of a ruin, and he concocts a plan to win her heart.

Gabriel's old-fashioned courtship touches something deep inside Kassie and, although struggling to believe someone as handsome as Gabriel could possibly be interested in her, she soon realises she has fallen irrevocably in love with him. However, just as Kassie shares everything of herself with Gabriel, her world comes crashing down.

Can their romance survive or will it fall in ruins, like the relics of antiquity that brought them together.

All At Once It's You

When Alex arrives in the small village of Rosedale Abbey, to take up a position as a research assistant for a renowned archaeologist, the last thing she is looking for, or expects to find, is love.

Jake was perfectly happy with the status quo. When it came to relationships, he didn't do committed or long term. He called the shots, and if his current flame didn't like it, she knew what to do. A philosophy, which served him well - until he met Alex.

Romance blooms, but even as the untamed wilderness of the North Yorkshire moors weaves its spell, a long-buried secret might yet jeopardise their happily ever after.

Cobweb Dreams

A Novella

A holiday on the Scottish isle of Mull was just the break Chloe Shepherd needed, an escape from her boring office job and her complete lack of anything resembling a social life. Romance, it seems, isn't on the cards and, although Chloe dreams of finding her soulmate she is beginning to believe love is like cobwebs — spun overnight, only to vanish in the early morning breeze.

Under sufferance, Dominic Winters makes a flying visit to Mull to check on a rental property owned by his family. He hasn't got time for this — so indulging in a holiday fling is the last thing on his mind.

A lamb stuck in a bog proves a most unexpected matchmaker and, while Mull weaves its magic, Chloe wonders whether those fragile cobwebs might be far more stubborn than she thought.

Just One Step

A Short Story

In the aftermath of an horrific car accident, Daisy Forrester travels to Italy - hoping, so far from her memories, she might begin to heal.

Archaeologist, and single father, Adam Willoughby is too busy looking after his young daughter to give romance let alone love, a thought.

Neither expects a chance encounter in an ancient ruin to be anything more, but sometimes, that's all it takes.

His Heart's Second Sigh

A Novella

Reuben Faulkner and Paige Latimer are two happily single people, who have no desire to upset the status quo.

Unexpectedly, they are thrown together, only to discover both want far more than a casual friendship.

Just when things take an interesting turn, Reuben's past catches up with them, and threatens to derail their blossoming romance before it has chance to start.